THE SEVEN WONDERS
OF THE MODERN WORLD

THE
TAJ MAHAL

BY SARA GREEN

BELLWETHER MEDIA • MINNEAPOLIS, MN

Blastoff! Discovery launches a new mission: reading to learn. Filled with facts and features, each book offers you an exciting new world to explore!

BLASTOFF! UNIVERSE

BLASTOFF! Beginners
GRADE K

BLASTOFF! READERS
GRADES 1-3

BLASTOFF! DISCOVERY
GRADE 4

This edition first published in 2021 by Bellwether Media, Inc.

No part of this publication may be reproduced in whole or in part without written permission of the publisher. For information regarding permission, write to Bellwether Media, Inc., Attention: Permissions Department, 6012 Blue Circle Drive, Minnetonka, MN 55343.

Library of Congress Cataloging-in-Publication Data

Names: Green, Sara, 1964- author.
Title: The Taj Mahal / by Sara Green.
Description: Minneapolis, MN : Bellwether Media, Inc., 2021. |
Series: Blastoff! discovery: The seven wonders of the modern world |
    Includes bibliographical references and index. | Audience: Ages
    7-13 | Audience: Grades 4-6 | Summary: "Engaging images
    accompany information about the Taj Mahal. The combination of
    high-interest subject matter and narrative text is intended for
    students in grades 3 through 8"–Provided by publisher"– Provided
    by publisher.
Identifiers: LCCN 2020018890 (print) | LCCN 2020018891 (ebook)
    | ISBN 9781644872710 (library binding) | ISBN
    9781681037349 (ebook)
Subjects: LCSH: Taj Mahal (Agra, India)–Juvenile literature. |
    Mausoleums–India–Agra–Juvenile literature. | Agra (India)–
    Buildings, structures, etc.–Juvenile literature.
Classification: LCC DS486.A3 G73 2021 (print) | LCC DS486.A3
    (ebook) | DDC 954.02/57092–dc23
LC record available at https://lccn.loc.gov/2020018890
LC ebook record available at https://lccn.loc.gov/2020018891

Editor: Betsy Rathburn   Designer: Brittany McIntosh

Printed in the United States of America, North Mankato, MN.

TABLE OF CONTENTS

A MARBLE MARVEL

Welcome to Agra! This city in northern India is home to the Taj Mahal. It is one of the world's most famous monuments. You cannot wait to see it in person!

You arrive at the entrance called the Great Gate. This entrance welcomes thousands of visitors each day. Here, you catch your first view of the monument. The white marble dome shimmers in the sunlight. A long pool reflects its image. The Taj Mahal is even more beautiful than you imagined!

WHAT IS THE TAJ MAHAL?

CENOTAPHS

The tombs inside the Taj Mahal that are visible to the public are called cenotaphs. They are empty. The real tombs of Shah Jahān and Mumtaz Mahal are beneath the monument.

The Taj Mahal is a **mausoleum** in Agra, India. The monument sits on the Yamuna River. It contains the tombs of the Mughal emperor Shah Jahān and his wife, Mumtaz Mahal.

The Taj Mahal is famous for its white marble. Ornamental **inlays** made with gemstones are pressed into the marble. The monument's most recognized feature is its onion-shaped dome. It reaches a height of over 200 feet (61 meters) tall.

INLAY

WHERE IS THE TAJ MAHAL?

TAJ MAHAL
AGRA, INDIA

N
W E
S

The Taj Mahal **complex** spans 42 acres (17 hectares). It includes gardens, **canals**, and fountains. Four towers called **minarets** surround the Taj Mahal. They were built with a slight outward lean to protect the monument. If the minarets collapse, they will fall away from the building.

MINARET

THINK ABOUT IT

Why would symmetry have mattered to the designers of the Taj Mahal?

A red sandstone building sits on each side of the Taj Mahal. One is a **mosque**. The other served as a guest house. The two identical buildings create **symmetry**. Examples of symmetry are found throughout the complex. Both halves of the monument mirror each other!

MOSQUE

A LABOR OF LOVE

The Mughal Empire began in 1526. It lasted more than 300 years. At its peak, it ruled most of India, Pakistan, and Afghanistan. The empire was wealthy and powerful. Shah Jahān was its fifth emperor. His rule began in 1628.

SHAH JAHĀN

SHAH JAHĀN WITH MUMTAZ MAHAL

Years before Shah Jahān's rule began, he met Arjumand Banu at a royal **bazaar** in 1607. The two fell in love. They were married five years later. Shah Jahān gave his wife the title Mumtaz Mahal. Mumtaz Mahal was Shah Jahān's constant companion. She even traveled with him into battles!

Mumtaz Mahal died in 1631 after giving birth to her fourteenth child. Shah Jahān was heartbroken. He built the Taj Mahal as a tomb for his beloved wife. Construction on the tomb began in 1632. It was completed in 1648. The rest of the complex was finished five years later.

Materials from around the world were brought in to build the monument. More than 40 types of gemstones arrived from Asia and Europe. They were pressed into the marble to make beautiful designs. This method is called *parchin kari.*

PARCHIN KARI

1. Artists made drawings on marble. They chiseled out the shapes.

2. Artists chose gemstones based on color. They used grindstones and chisels to shape them.

3. Artists polished the gemstones and glued them into place.

TAJ MAHAL TIMELINE

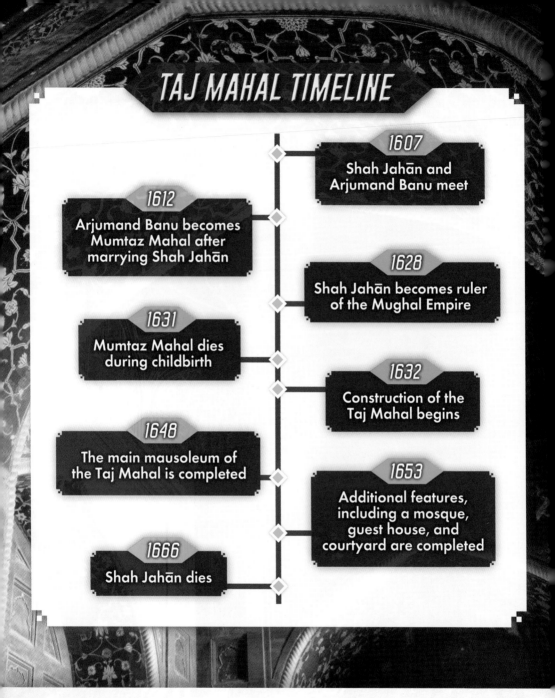

1607
Shah Jahān and Arjumand Banu meet

1612
Arjumand Banu becomes Mumtaz Mahal after marrying Shah Jahān

1628
Shah Jahān becomes ruler of the Mughal Empire

1631
Mumtaz Mahal dies during childbirth

1632
Construction of the Taj Mahal begins

1648
The main mausoleum of the Taj Mahal is completed

1653
Additional features, including a mosque, guest house, and courtyard are completed

1666
Shah Jahān dies

More than 20,000 skilled workers moved to Agra to work on the project. They included stonecutters and **calligraphers**.

Bricks and marble were used to build the Taj Mahal. Animals hauled marble blocks from a **quarry** hundreds of miles away. Workers built a long dirt ramp through Agra to reach the site. Animals pulled cartloads of supplies up the ramp to the tomb. **Pulleys** raised the materials into position.

MAKRANA MARBLE QUARRY, WHERE TAJ MAHAL STONE WAS MINED

RESTORE AND PROTECT

In 1658, control of the Mughal Empire changed hands. Shah Jahān's son Aurangzeb overthrew him and imprisoned him in Agra. Shah Jahān died in 1666. He was buried next to his wife in the Taj Mahal.

AURANGZEB

TAJ MAHAL IN THE 1700s

Aurangzeb ruled the Mughal Empire until 1707. He neglected the Taj Mahal. Its buildings and gardens fell into disrepair. **Vandals** caused further damage. They damaged the marble walls and stole precious gems.

THINK ABOUT IT

Why did Lord Curzon care so deeply about the Taj Mahal?

RESTORATION OF THE TAJ MAHAL

The British took control of India from the Mughal Empire in 1858. Britain's Lord Curzon admired India's artistic and **cultural** history. He fought plans to tear down the Taj Mahal. Instead, he ordered a major **restoration** of the complex.

LORD CURZON

Starting around 1900, Lord Curzon began repairing the buildings. He restored the canals and remodeled the gardens. Work finished in 1908.

A GLIMPSE OF THE PAST

The Taj Mahal appears almost exactly as it was designed in 1631. Only the gardens have changed.

TAJ MAHAL
DURING WORLD WAR II

The Taj Mahal was not out of danger. War threatened
its destruction. The British government took measures to
protect the monument during World War II. Workers built
scaffolding to protect it from air attacks.

In 1947, India gained independence from the British. But troubles followed. War broke out with Pakistan in 1965. Once again, scaffolding was built to protect the Taj Mahal from bombers. By this time, the Taj Mahal had become one of the world's greatest **tourist** attractions.

THEN AND NOW

THEN

Workers built scaffolding made of bricks to reach the Taj Mahal's dome. At the time, scaffolding was usually made from bamboo. Brick took much longer to build!

NOW

Today, metal scaffolding is used to clean and repair parts of the Taj Mahal. But bamboo scaffolding is still sometimes used for work on the dome!

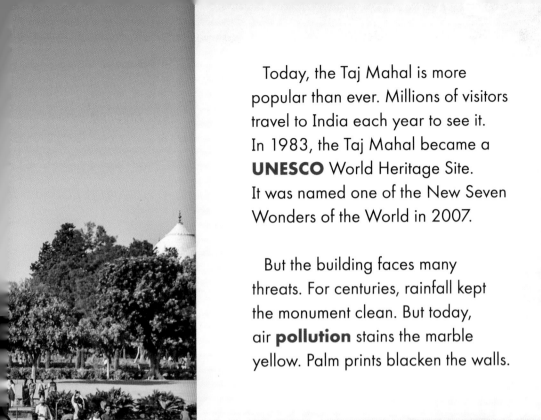

Today, the Taj Mahal is more popular than ever. Millions of visitors travel to India each year to see it. In 1983, the Taj Mahal became a **UNESCO** World Heritage Site. It was named one of the New Seven Wonders of the World in 2007.

But the building faces many threats. For centuries, rainfall kept the monument clean. But today, air **pollution** stains the marble yellow. Palm prints blacken the walls.

TAJ MAHAL SURROUNDED BY SMOG CAUSED BY AIR POLLUTION

The Yamuna River also affects the Taj Mahal. The building's **foundation** needs moisture from the river to stay strong. But the river is drying out. Without it, the foundation could shrink and crack. Some people fear the Taj Mahal could sink into the riverbed.

THINK ABOUT IT

Why is the Yamuna River important to the past, present, and future of the Taj Mahal?

YAMUNA RIVER

Sewage and trash in the river attract millions of insects to the area. They settle on the Taj Mahal's marble walls. Their waste turns the walls green!

People have found new ways to clean the monument. Workers apply mud to the marble walls. The mud sucks in dust and dirt. After the mud dries, workers wash it off with clean water. The marble is left sparkling white!

The Indian government has also made changes to reduce pollution. Cars are not allowed in the area. Nearby factories have been closed. Vans containing air purifiers are parked near the Taj Mahal. They help clean the air!

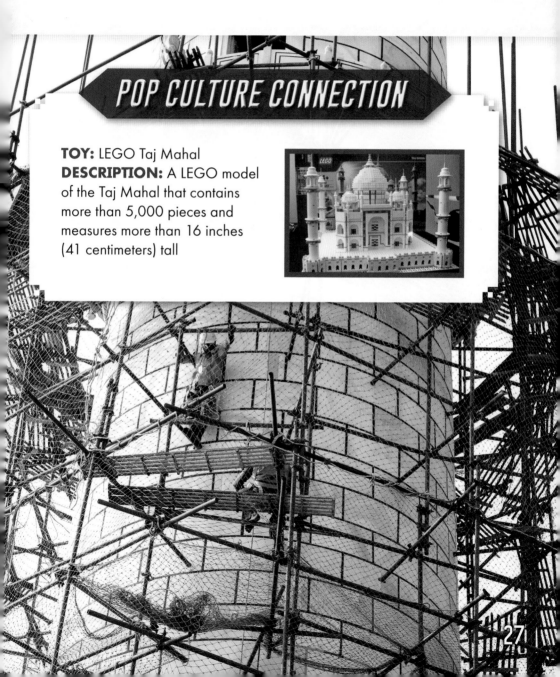

POP CULTURE CONNECTION

TOY: LEGO Taj Mahal
DESCRIPTION: A LEGO model of the Taj Mahal that contains more than 5,000 pieces and measures more than 16 inches (41 centimeters) tall

Archaeologists continue to research the Taj Mahal. In 2014, a team uncovered the remains of a palace and gardens across the river. These gardens grow the same kinds of flowers and trees the Mughals once planted there!

COMPARE AND CONTRAST

THE TAJ MAHAL

THE WHITE HOUSE

THE TAJ MAHAL	THE WHITE HOUSE
LOCATION India	**LOCATION** United States
PURPOSE mausoleum for Mumtaz Mahal and Shah Jahān	**PURPOSE** residence and workplace of the president of the United States
BUILT 1632 to 1653	**BUILT** 1792 to around 1800
BUILDING MATERIALS white marble, red sandstone	**BUILDING MATERIALS** sandstone
COST more than $800 million	**COST** $3.5 million
SIZE 34,596 square feet (3,214 square meters)	**SIZE** 54,900 square feet (5,100 square meters)

CHANGING COLORS

The Taj Mahal changes colors according to the time of day. It appears pink in the morning and white during the day. The building is gold in the moonlight.

Today, experts are committed to protecting the Taj Mahal complex. With their support, this wonder will amaze and inspire people for years to come!

GLOSSARY

archaeologists—scientists who study things left behind by ancient people

bazaar—a marketplace that has rows of small shops selling many kinds of goods

calligraphers—artists who make beautiful handwriting

canals—human-made waterways that drain or irrigate land or help people get around

complex—buildings and grounds that make up a place

cultural—the customary beliefs, values, and traditions of a racial, religious, or social group

foundation—a base or support on top of which a structure is built

inlays—decorations that have been set into a surface

mausoleum—a tomb or building where someone is buried

minarets—tall, thin towers attached to a mosque; minarets have balconies used to call people to prayers.

mosque—a place of worship for followers of the Islam religion

pollution—the presence of harmful materials in the environment

pulleys—simple machines used to lift heavy objects; a pulley consists of a rope fitted inside a grooved wheel.

quarry—a place from which rocks are dug for use in building

restoration—the act of returning something to its original condition

scaffolding—a series of raised platforms, or scaffolds, built as support for workers and their tools and materials

sewage—wastewater

symmetry—a visual technique where the right side of an object looks the same as its left side

tourist—related to people who travel to visit a place

UNESCO—the United Nations Educational, Scientific and Cultural Organization; UNESCO works to educate people and preserve world landmarks.

vandals—people who destroy or damage property on purpose

TO LEARN MORE

AT THE LIBRARY

Green, Sara. *Ancient India*. Minneapolis, Minn.:
Bellwether Media, 2020.

Murray, Laura K. *Engineering the Taj Mahal*. Edina,
Minn.: Abdo Publishing, 2018.

Oachs, Emily Rose. *India*. Minneapolis, Minn.:
Bellwether Media, 2018.

ON THE WEB

FACTSURFER

Factsurfer.com gives you
a safe, fun way to find
more information.

1. Go to www.factsurfer.com.

2. Enter "Taj Mahal" into the search box
   and click Q.

3. Select your book cover to see a list
   of related content.

INDEX